July, 2018

This Adventure belongs to:

Bailey

Love, Grandma

For my Sawyer and Story.
Always believe. See the magic. Follow your dreams.

© 2017 Elise Monsour Puckett
The Adventures of Scout and Kit: The Berry Patch
First Edition, September 2017

Roly Poly Books, Publishing Company
Christiansburg, VA, U.S.A

Editing: Shayla Eaton, ShaylaRaquel.com
Cover Design & Illustrations: Tessa Riley
Interior Formatting: Elise Monsour Puckett, EliseMonsourPuckett.com

The illustrations in this book were created with Prismacolor Premier pencils on watercolor paper.
Text set in Adobe InDesign

ISBN 978-0-9994391-0-4

THE ADVENTURES OF
Scout & Kit
The BERRY Patch

By: Elise Monsour Puckett

Illustrated By: Tessa Riley

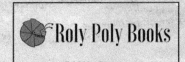
Roly Poly Books
Publishing Company

Adventure Awaits!

The sun was awake and giggles poured from the attic. It was Scout and Kit. They were brother and sister and had big imaginations. They loved to play make-believe games full of knights and dragons, princesses and fairies, wizards and gnomes, wardrobes and attics. Each adventure was full of magic!

That morning, they headed out together to explore. From their treehouse window, they noticed their flowers had been bitten by frost. Scout and Kit loved to pick flowers for their mommy, but these scraggly ones just wouldn't do. They would just have to pick flowers somewhere else.

They wandered over the hill and down the lane and into the forest. Along with the flowers, they collected sticks, rocks, pinecones, and all sorts of outdoor treasures. Suddenly, they happened upon a peculiar stone wall. It was gray, smudged with dirt and covered in weeds and flowers.

They followed the wall to see where it led
and found an old wooden door.
But it was locked!

Disappointed that they couldn't peek
inside, Scout and Kit turned to
walk away when they heard a
clink-clank sound.

Curious, they searched through the overgrown weeds of the forest floor and there it was. An antique key covered in dirt and moss. They looked at each other full to the brim with wonder as they cleaned off the key. Scout placed the key in the hole, Kit turned the knob, and together they pushed the door open.

They couldn't believe their eyes. The garden beckoned them in.
What was this magical place?

They took a step inside and heard the chitter-chatter of
some playful squirrels and then the pitter-patter of some tiny feet.
That's when Scout felt a tap-tap on his shoe.

Scout and Kit looked down and to their surprise, they saw a little mouse with a cane and a floppy hat. He wore a vest with tattered patches and mismatched buttons.

"Hi, my name is Henry," said the mouse. "What are your names?" They were speechless. Could that mouse really be talking?

"Uh-uh, my name is Scout and this is my little sister Kit," stuttered Scout.

"Nice to meet you," said Henry. "Now come along. I haven't got all day."

"Where are we going?" asked Kit.

"To see the berry patch!"

BERRIES

Their first stop was the blackberries. Henry explained that they look like clusters of round bubbles filled with purple juice.

"Each bite is a surprise because they are sometimes sweet and sometimes tart, but always delicious," Henry said.

Next, Henry showed them the strawberry patch. "Strawberries are red and shaped like hearts. They have tiny edible seeds that crunch a little when you chew them."

Moving along, Henry guided Scout and Kit to the blueberry bushes.
"Blueberries are round and dark blue or purple," described Henry.
They watched Henry stuff both of his cheeks full.

Raspberries were their next stop. It was hard to hear Henry speak, as he kept nibbling on *everything* in sight, but with his mouth full, he told them that raspberries look like blackberries but are smaller and dark pink or red.

Giggling, Scout and Kit placed raspberries on the tips of each finger and wiggled them all around.

"Hey, what are those twisty vines over there?" asked Scout.

"Follow me, and I'll show you!" exclaimed Henry.

Henry led Scout and Kit into what seemed like a cave made out of vines. It was grim and dark with small rays of sunlight shining in between the vines. Once inside, they were surrounded by oodles of purple grapes. Henry picked one. "Be careful," said Henry. "Some grapes have seeds in them." He spit one out on the ground. "Grapes can be red, purple, dark blue, or green."

"What's that buzzing sound?" Kit asked.

"Oh no!" Henry muttered. "Bees! Run!"

And off they went, as fast as their little legs (and mouse legs) could carry them. Darting this way and that way, going over logs and under tree branches, jumping over thickets, dodging the prickly thistles, and finally ending up at the other end of the berry patch.

"Whew! I think we lost them," Scout said, out of breath.

"Yeah, but where are we?" asked Kit as she sat down on a sturdy toadstool for a rest.

"Well, at the cloudberries, of course!" Henry exclaimed. Cloudberries look like raspberries but are orange or yellow," Henry said. "Cloudberries are tart, and caterpillars love to eat their leaves."

"Wow! Look over there," Kit shouted to Scout. They were down by the waterhole.

Scout and Kit followed Henry as he jumped across some flat rocks in the water. Swimming around them were colorful fishies, salamanders, and tadpoles. Toads hopped nearby, silly snails rested on top of river rocks, and roly-polies hid beneath them.

Tiny gnome houses filled the trees and their lights shone from the windows.

"Henry, Henry!" exclaimed a mousy voice. "Where are you?"

It was Henry's wife, Judy Mouse. "Oh, there you are, dear," she said as she handed him an acorn cup and saucer filled with berry tea. Judy Mouse reached over and picked a honeysuckle from a nearby bush, pulled off the bottom, and plopped a single drop of honey into Henry's tea.

"Henry, it's time for supper," she said as she pulled back a big maple leaf. Behind the leaf was their little mouse family sitting down for tea with toast and strawberry jam.

"One last thing before I go," Henry said as he pointed over to the Wild Wood. "This is very important. So, listen carefully. Some berries are poisonous and can make you sick. Never pick or eat a wild berry unless your mommy or daddy says it is ok. Promise you will follow this *berry* important rule?"

"Oh, yes!" promised Scout and Kit.

"Do you pinkie swear?" asked Henry.

"We pinkie swear," answered Scout and Kit. And that was that. Henry gave them each a packet of berry seeds so they could plant them in their very own garden, and sent them on their way.

The sun was setting and lightning bugs were starting to peek out and twinkle in the trees. Scout and Kit ran straight home to tell their parents about their adventure and get to work on growing a delicious berry patch of their own.

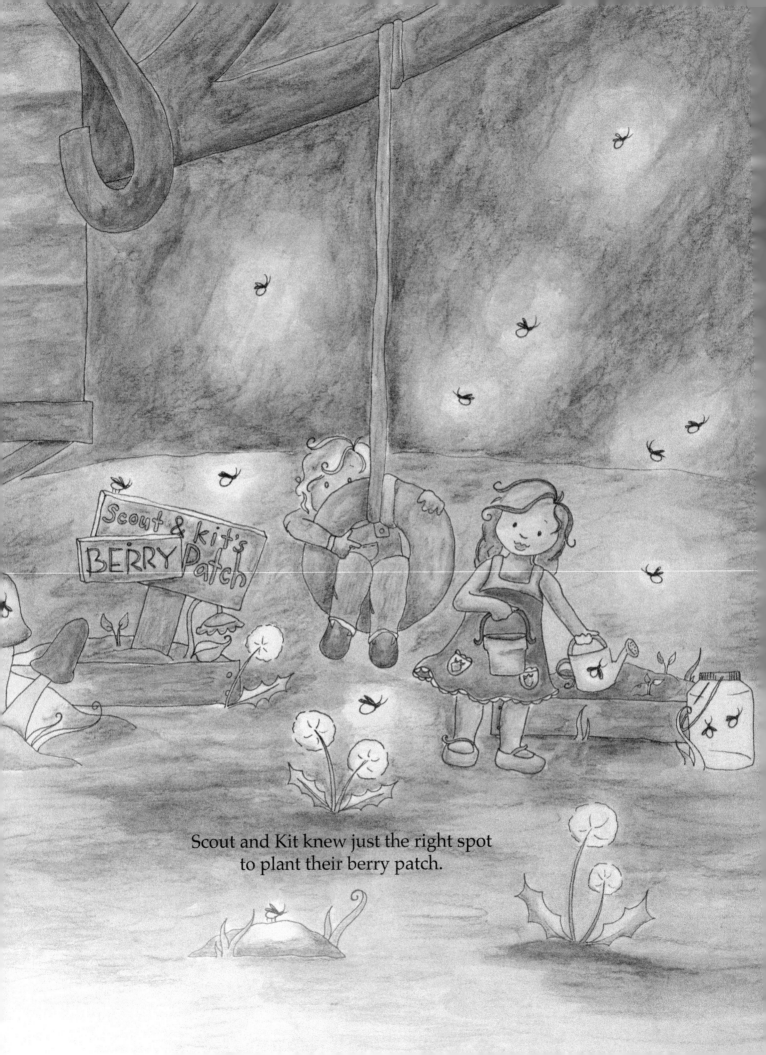

Scout and Kit knew just the right spot
to plant their berry patch.

"A child's playground is as big as their imagination."
—Judy Monsour, Mother of the Author

The End

About the Author

Elise takes her tea with a dollop of fresh honey.

Elise Monsour Puckett is a graduate of Roanoke College with a bachelor's degree in Business Administration. Elise is a writer, author, poet, and storyteller (to her children). She grew up in the little town of Salem, Virginia, and now lives nestled in the foothills of the Appalachian Mountains.

Elise is happily married to a spitfire redhead and is the mother of two beautiful, silly children with great, big imaginations! She gets her inspiration from her children, nature, her inventive father, and her mother, whose dream is to write children's books and poetry.

In her children's playroom is where she does most of her writing, but Elise also enjoys creating her stories while sitting on a picnic blanket outside on a beautiful summer day, and while watching her children catch lightning bugs on sweet summer nights.

It is Elise's dream that her stories bring smiles to the faces of children everywhere and sprinkle each child's day with a little bit of magic when reading her books.

About the Illustrator

Tessa Riley is the talented illustrator behind The Adventures of Scout and Kit children's book series. The whimsical details in her art are one of the many reasons Elise handpicked her to illustrate these magical books.

Born in Georgia, Tessa then moved to Missouri, where she spent ten years of her childhood. She now lives in Blacksburg, Virginia, and will be a Virginia Tech graduate (Class of 2018) with a bachelor's degree in Visual Communication Design and a minor in Art History.

Tessa loves the outdoors and hiking with her dog, Roadie. She also enjoys running cross-country and is a former track athlete for Virginia Tech. One of Tessa's passions is traveling and she had quite the adventure on her most recent excursion to Alaska, where she ate cloudberries and went hiking in Denali.

For more information about Elise Monsour Puckett and her books, please visit elisemonsourpuckett.com

CPSIA information can be obtained
at www.ICGtesting.com
Printed in the USA
BVOW07s0049161117
500545BV00002B/7/P

9 780999 439104